Today I Feel Silly

& Other MOODS That Make My Day

by Jamie Lee Curtis

illustrated by Laura Cornell

SCHOLASTIC INC.

New York Toronto London Auckland Sydney
Mexico City New Delhi Hong Kong

Thanks to the three "moodsketeers"—
Joanna, Phyllis and Laura.
And special thanks to Annie, for fixing the end.

ISBN 0-439-15313-1

Text copyright © 1998 by Jamie Lee Curtis. Illustrations copyright © 1998 by Laura Cornell.
All rights reserved. Published by Scholastic Inc., 555 Broadway, New York, NY 10012, by arrangement with HarperCollins Publishers.
SCHOLASTIC and associated logos are trademarks and/or registered trademarks of Scholastic Inc.

12 11 10 9 8 7 6 5 4 3 2 1   9/9 0 1 2 3 4/0

Printed in China   50
First Scholastic printing, September 1999
Designed by Alicia Mikles

To my sister, Kelly,
who reminds me to do my smile exercises every day.
—J.L.C.

To Glenna
—L.C.

Today I feel silly.
Mom says it's the heat.
I put rouge on the cat
and gloves on my feet.
I ate noodles for breakfast
and pancakes at night.
I dressed like a star
and was quite a sight.

Today my mood's bad. I feel grumpy and mean.
I picked up my room. It still isn't clean.
I forgot to feed Franny and water the fern.
And the cocoa I'm making is starting to burn.

Today I am angry. You'd better stay clear.
My face is all pinched and red ear to ear.

My friends had a play date. They left me out.
My feelings are hurt. I want to shout!

Today I am joyful. My mood is first-rate.
My friend's sleeping over, she said she can't wait.
My freckles are popping, the sun is so bright.
I ran in the relay with all of my might.

BABY SWING

SCARY SLIDE

MOOD SWING

HYPERACTIVE STRAIGHT-A-WAY

Today I'm confused, my life's getting hairy.
Sam says he's my boyfriend but he also likes Mary.
My mom told my father he might be a dad.
I might get a brother. I'm not sure I'm glad.

Today I am quiet, my mom understands.
She gave me two ice creams and then we held hands.

We went to the movies and then had a bite.
I cried just a little and then felt all right.

Today I'm excited there's so much to do.
I'm going to sell cookies and lemonade too.

I'm starting a club to go clean up the park.

And I've got a big crush on my teacher named Mark.

Today I am cranky
so nothing seems right.
I have diarrhea
and broke my new kite.

Mom dyed her hair orange.

My dad shaved his beard.

My tooth came in crooked.
This family is weird.

Today I am lonely. I feel so small.
My Auntie's away. I wish that she'd call.
My mom's working late and my dad has the flu.
And although I've got stuff I've got nothing to do.

Today I am happy. I'm walking on air.

I learned how to knit

and to French-braid my hair.

I did my first solo in hip-hop and jazz.

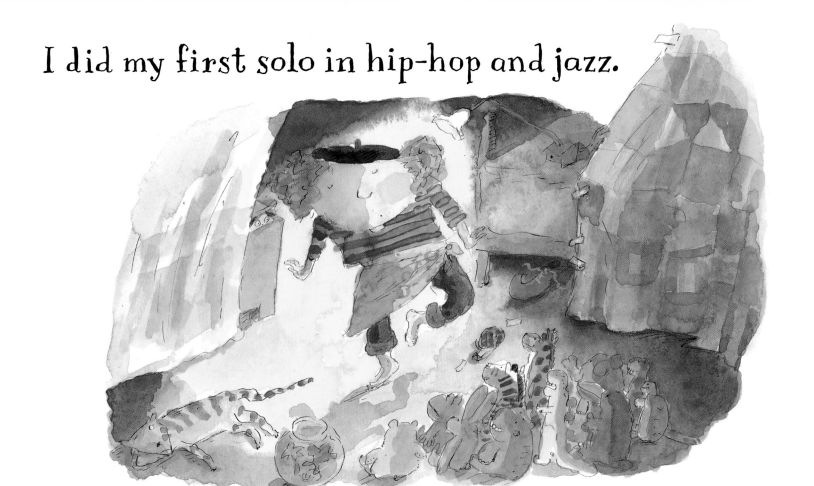

This day's been so great, I am full of pizzazz.

Today I'm discouraged and frustrated—see?
I tried Rollerblading and fell on my knee.
I really want straight hair,
but mine's curly-q.
Should I cut it or grow it,
oh what should I do?

Today I am sad, my mood's heavy and gray.
There's a frown on my face and it's been there all day.
My best friend and I had a really big fight.
She said that I tattled and I know that she's right.

Today my mood's great, it's the absolute best.
I rode a two-wheeler and passed my math test.
I played soccer at recess and we won the game.
I sang in the show and my parents both came.

I'd rather feel silly, excited or glad,
than cranky or grumpy, discouraged or sad.
But moods are just something that happen each day.
Whatever I'm feeling inside is okay!

How do YOU
feel today? . . .